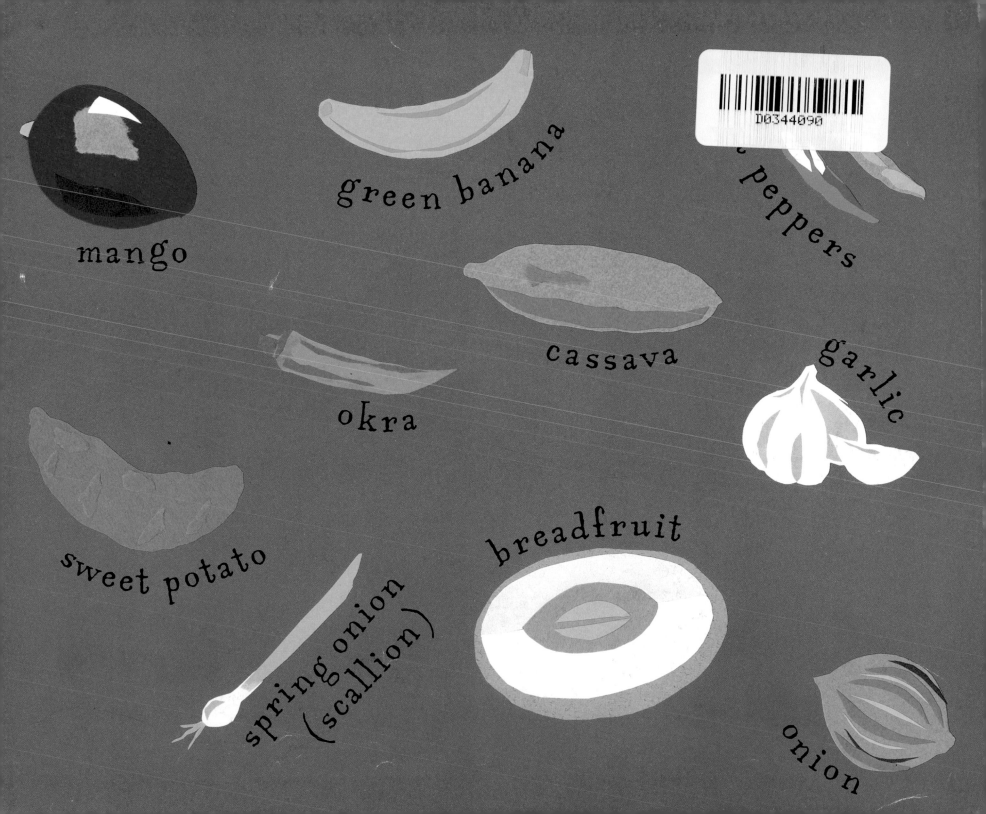

mango

green banana

peppers

cassava

garlic

okra

sweet potato

spring onion
(scallion)

breadfruit

onion

For Leila and Ian – PS
For Marcus, Michelle and Jay – AA

1 3 5 7 9 10 8 6 4 2

Text copyright © Pauline Stewart 2002
Illustrations copyright © Alex Ayliffe 2002

The rights of Pauline Stewart and Alex Ayliffe to be identified as the author and illustrator of this work have been
asserted by them in accordance with the Copyright, Designs and Patents Act, 1988.

First published in the United Kingdom in 2002 by
The Bodley Head Children's Books,
Random House, 20 Vauxhall Bridge Road, London SW1V 2SA

Random House Australia (Pty) Limited
20 Alfred Street, Milsons Point, Sydney
New South Wales 2061, Australia

Random House New Zealand Limited
18 Poland Road, Glenfield
Auckland 10, New Zealand

Random House South Africa (Pty) Limited
Endulini, 5a Jubilee Road,
Parktown 2193, South Africa

THE RANDOM HOUSE GROUP Limited Reg. No. 954009
www.randomhouse.co.uk

Papers used by Random House are natural, recyclable products made from
wood grown in sustainable forests. The manufacturing processes conform
to the environmental regulations of the country of origin.

A CIP catalogue record for this book is available from the British Library.

ISBN 0 370 32583 4

Printed in Singapore

What's in the Pan, Man?

Written by Pauline Stewart

Illustrated by Alex Ayliffe

THE BODLEY HEAD
LONDON

"Dan can cook man, without a cookbook.
He has a gourmet's hand!"
"Hmmmmmmm!" says Buecy.
"Something smells juicy."
"Bet you can't guess," dares Dan.
"Put me to the test man.
Lift the lid a little.
Bet you I can!"

"Wow that smells good man.
You cook even better than my gran –
sharp and sweet!
Onion, scallion, garlic and tomatoes?
Don't forget the thyme. In it goes!"

"Come, Dan, and size up our catch.
I don't think you'll find anything to match:
kingfish, bonito, red snapper,
Spanish mackerel, flying fish, lobster –
Take your pick quick, man, quick!"

"I'll have these please,"
says Dan putting three fish into the pan.

The fire licked the pot!
The water was bubbling hot hot!
And such a smell was held in the breeze,
it carried way past the palm trees!

Even the tourists in the Big Hotel
couldn't ignore the delicious smell.

Everyone came . . .
There was a stampede from the bus -
from the market square there came a rush!
Stray dogs came hoping for scraps;
babies were woken from their naps.

While Dan squeezed in more lime,
in quick time,
the whole town had formed a snaking line.
Along the beach they came from near and far,
some as far away as St Croix!

They cried:

"WHAT'S IN THE PAN, MAN?!"
"If you want to know –
then give me a hand!"
laughed Dan.

Everybody did ...
Janet who was jogging past
crushed the garlic fast fast.

Miss Doris dropped in ginger.
Miss Ethel and Mr Molloy diced up okra,
or 'ladies' fingers', if you prefer ...

Ashley poured in more water
Petra put in a pinch of sea salt
The twins put in two types of pepper.
Dan smiled, "That's much better!"

José began to beat out a tune
with a Dutch pot spoon.
There was roast breadfruit and corn,
burnt yellow,
and pink crunchy shrimps, clever fellow.

The smell made everyone giddy –
Until Dan shouted:

"EVERYTHING'S READY!!!"

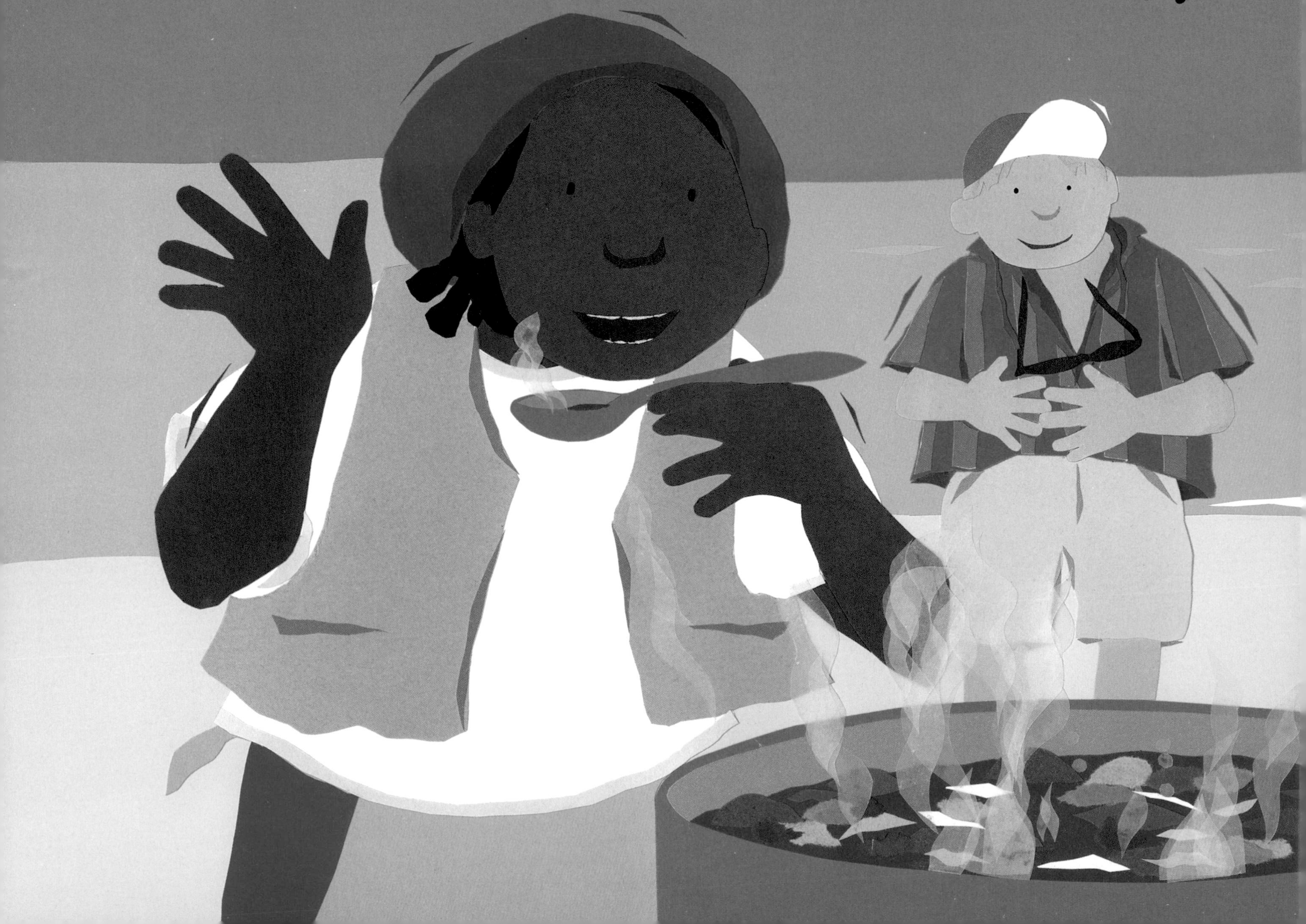

"Yummy!" said George, rubbing his tummy.
"Glorious!" sighed Pastor Smith, licking his lips.
"Yes sir!" said Eva swinging her hips.

They all ate right there
on the beach,
some sat on rocks,
most on their feet.

It wasn't quite a soup, it was some sort of stew.
A kind of gumbo – no recipe they knew.
And believe you me they'd tasted a few!

Dan grinned wide, man,
his teeth as bright as the frothing tide,
but . . . there came a Dickens of a roar:

"PLEASE COULD WE HAVE SOME MORE?!"

Dan peered inside the pot,
his dinner guests had scoffed the lot:

"There's no more, man . . .
Sorry –EMPTY PAN!"

lime

peppers

coconut

pineapple

aubergine

thyme

papaya

cho-cho

tomato

ginger